My mommy

is in America and she met Buffalo Bill

Jean Regnaud & Émile Bravo

My mommy

is in America and she met Buffalo Bill

FANFARE · PONENT MON

Chapter 1: Madame Moinot
It's the first day at the big kids' school and we're waiting for the teacher outside the classroom.

That's it,
here she is!

...

Shoot... Why's my teacher's so ugly? And on top of that, she doesn't look very kind...

The teacher asks us to line up two-by-two.
All of the others take a classmate's hand...
Me, I remain alone. I don't know anyone because last year I went to kindergarten in another neighborhood.

There's another kid who's all alone near me. He comes and takes my hand.

That's it, we're all lined up two-by-two. We can go in now.

When we're all sitting, the teacher introduces herself. Her name is Madame Moinot. She writes her name on the board... At least I think that's her name because I can't read yet.

The teacher asks us our names and what our parents do. The first kids answer and the teacher writes in a huge notebook.

My socks are getting all sweaty. I don't want it to be my turn. I want time to stop. WHAT IF I RUN AWAY!!!

I'm all red and feel horribly hot. What am I going to say my Mommy does? My ears are buzzing and my head is throbbing. It's already the turn of the boy next to me!

His name is Alain...

...his Mommy is a nurse and his Daddy paints lead soldiers.

That makes everyone laugh.
Monday, September 14, 1970
?

The teacher isn't happy. She says it's not nice to laugh at someone. She tells us to stop laughing and be quiet.

I pray that she won't remember where she is any longer and will skip over me...

But she turns to me...

My throat is dry.

She asks me if the cat's got my tongue and then what my name is.

I unclench my teeth a little and I tell her:

MynameisJean- myDaddy'sa-boss-myMommy'sasecretary!

I say it so quickly that I'm sure no one understood. But the teacher has already turned to the next one.

I don't hear anyone else's responses, I am petrified. My feet and socks are soaking wet.

Monday
Afterwards, the teacher tells us that she is going to retire after Christmas and that another teacher will replace her. She's really sad when she tells us that.
Christmas seems so far away...

Interlude

Chapter 2: My Daddy
Mommies and Daddies come to pick their children up after school.

As for me, Yvette picks me up.

Yvette, is our nanny.
She lives with us. She fixes our meals, makes us do our homework, washes us in the morning, gets us dressed...

...and comes to pick us up after school.

My little brother Paul is in the car. He's a year younger than me and he's still in kindergarten.

Paul and I, we just adore each other and have our own way of letting it show.

To make us stop fighting, Yvette threatens that she won't let us have any iced chocolate milk.

It's a very effective threat because we love it when she gives us this treat.

Recipe for iced chocolate milk, by
Yvette
1
2
3
4
5

In the evening, after we've bickered, argued, fought, made up, slugged each other, chased around in every room, we bathe and have supper. In our house we say supper and not dinner. I must say, winter or summer, our evening meal starts with a soup or stew.

My favorite soup is the one that has numbers and letters.

Every evening, Yvette tries to teach us part of the alphabet.

My Daddy comes home late from work. It's not because of the distance, his factory is right next door to our house. It's because of his worries: he's the boss.

And it seems that, being the boss is a heck of a job as it makes you have lots of cares.

Cares make you glare. My Daddy is always glaring because of his cares.

There's one thing that keeps bugging me. Every evening I swear to myself I'm going to ask about it but I never dare. Tonight I'm going to.

It was Jean's first day at school today...

Ah yes, of course... So, everything okay?

Er... yes... I've a new friend called Alain

What's his surname?

Er... I dunno... I...

I do NOT know.

I-do-not-know-I-do-not-know-him-well-enough-yet.

And you, Paul? How did school go?
?
?

I fight with Jean.

I FOUGHT with Jean.

Oh, yes, that's right... Is there any more tomato salad?

What's the matter, Jean? Do you want to say something?

Where's my Mommy?

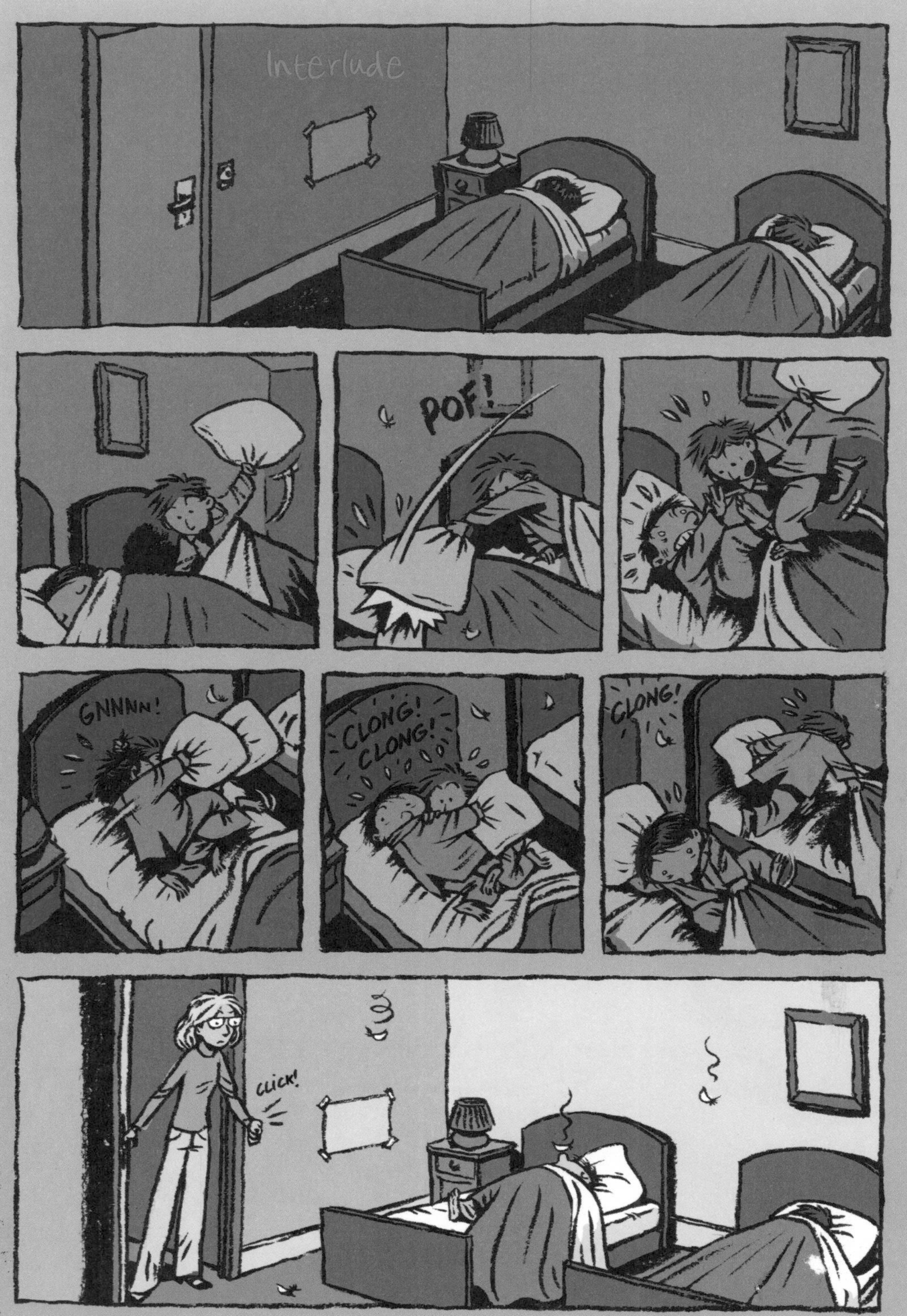
Interlude
POF!
GNNNN!
CLONG! CLONG!
CLONG!
CLICK!

Chapter 3: Michele
My neighbor's name is Michele Meunier
She's two years older than me.

Her parents have kennels. They're weird, especially her Daddy. He yells all the time...

...at his wife...

...or at Michele...

When he yells, the dogs get in a tizzy and start barking. So then he yells at the dogs who get even more worked up.

Sometimes everyone is screeching and yelling at the same time. It's impossible to tell who started it. They really make a terrible racket.

Some nights the dogs howl just like wolves.

According to Yvette, it means someone has just died. When she said that my Daddy just shrugged. He doesn't believe that.

My Daddy doesn't want me to play with Michele. He says that the dogs are dangerous. Michele's parents don't want her to play with me, I think they don't like my Daddy. So when we play together, we do it like this...

...each one on either side of the privet hedge which divides our yards.

Actually, Michele only plays with me when she's bored. When her friends come around, she's doesn't pay me any attention.

But, other than that, Michele is nice.
Then again, she's the only neighbor I have...

Sometimes, she wants to play hairdressers.
I brush her hair and she tells me all her girl stories.

But I'm not really into that.
I prefer it when we play Indians.

I saw you in the playground...
?

We're in the same school now...

Yes, but you're with the little ones.

No, I'm with the big kids!
The little ones at the big kids' school are still the little ones!
...

Can you read yet?
Only "A"

See, you're still one of the li'l ones... Hey! Not so hard!!

Sorry... I wish I knew how to write... so that...
So that, what?

So that, I can write to my Mommy.
...to your Mommy?!

Well, yeah, you know that she's away on a trip. If I write to her, she'll answer...
!!!

One afternoon, Michele waits for me at our meeting place.

She asks me if I can keep a secret... A BIG SECRET...

My heart is pounding very hard when I say yes. Very often secrets turn out to be nasty surprises. But this time it's a good one, one that's unbelievable!

Michele pulls a postcard from out under her sweater...

...she tells me that **MY MOMMY SENT IT!!!**

Michele looks me right in the eye and tells me that she's willing to read it to me but that first I must promise that I'll not tell a soul about this postcard.

And yet, my Daddy and my brother and Yvette would be happy to know that Mommy has written to me... but Michele warns me not to tell them. I ask Michele how come she got the postcard. She says that it's just because my Mommy doesn't want anyone to know that she's written to me...

Dear Jean. Everything's OK.
Today I am in Spain. It is very hot. The women play castanets and the men fight bulls. Yesterday, I had a very good paella with crayfish. Then I swam in the sea. It was nice and warm.
Lots of love. Mommy.

Interlude

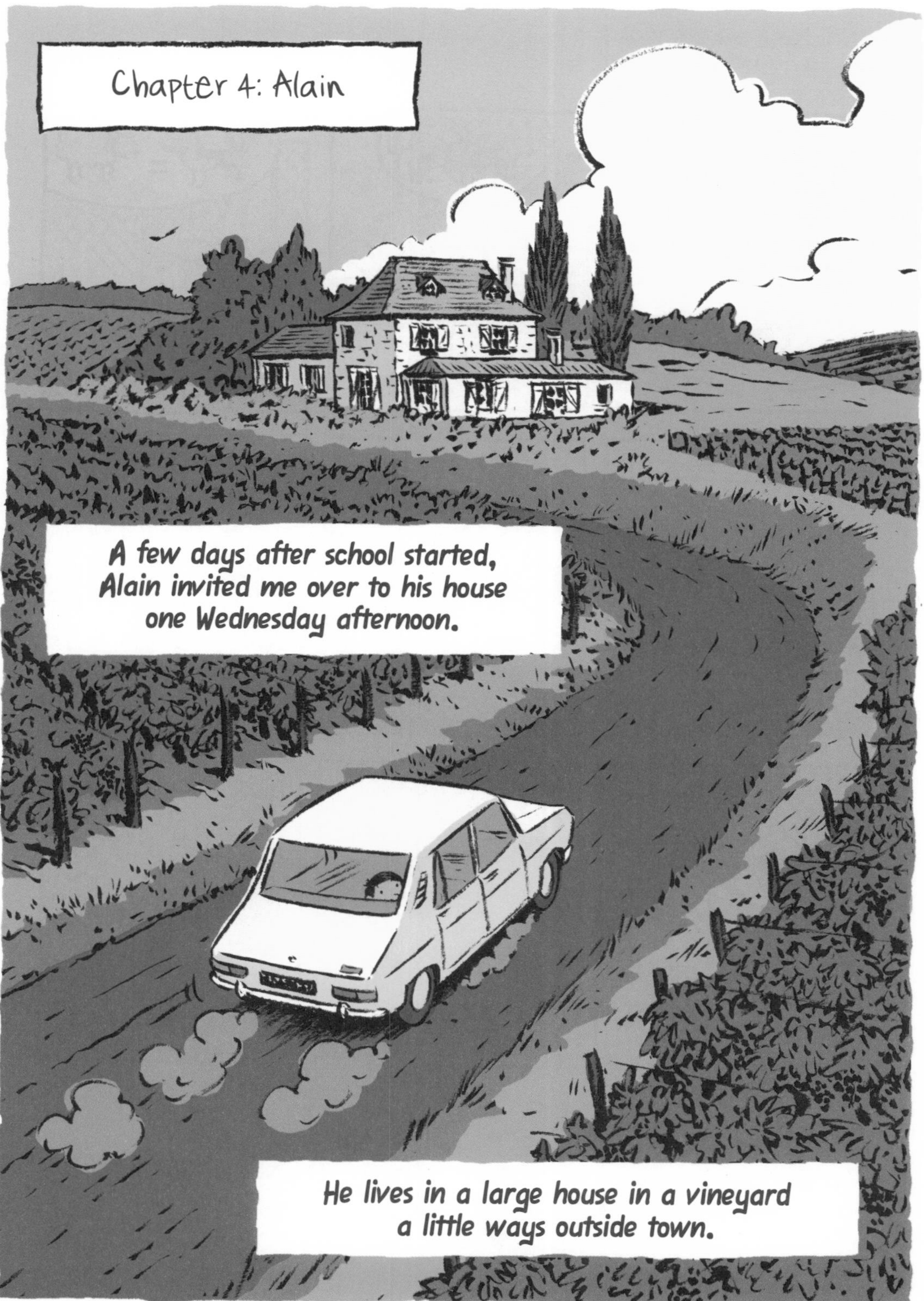
Chapter 4: Alain
A few days after school started,
Alain invited me over to his house
one Wednesday afternoon.
He lives in a large house in a vineyard
a little ways outside town.

Alain has a record player.
It's cool to be able to listen
to one's own records.

But he says that it's very fragile and he won't let me touch it.

Alain has loads of records but
he plays the same song over and
over again. It's one where some
guys are singing : "The Way
With Every Sailor"

I tell Alain that his Mommy is really pretty. He tells me that she's not his real Mommy because he's adopted...

His voice is real cheerful when he tells me. Like if he were saying "I love Oreos."

And d'you know your real Mommy?
No, I was adopted at birth.

What about your Mommy, what's she like?

I can't remember anymore. It's been a long time since I last saw her.
?

Are you adopted too?
?

No, well, I don't think so. It's just that she's away on a trip

Me too, I'm going to travel when I'm bigger!

Afterwards we go and see his Daddy. He really does paint lead soldiers.

But the weirdest thing is that he's got a big black beard and is in a wheelchair.

All around him, on shelves, there are dozens of little lead soldiers.

Marching with their rifles raised,

rolling canons,

charging on horses.

Alain's Daddy tells me what they are called. There are infantry, artillery and hussars...

There are even some called 'hairy ones'*!

He tells me to choose one to take home.

I'm not really into soldiers. I prefer cowboys and Indians. But I don't want to upset Alain's Daddy so I take a hussar on horseback.

*Poilu lit. "hairy" was the common name given to the French soldier during WWI and meant "courageous" or "brave" in common parlance of the time.

Alain's Mommy makes us a delicious snack. There's a big jar of Nutella. I often eat it at Granny Edith's, but at home it's a no-no.

I spread some on several slices of toast

Your Daddy's the manager of the bottling factory, isn't he?
Yes, ma'am.

What about your Mommy, what does she do?

She's a secretary.
?

But you told me your Mommy was away on a trip!
Yup, she's a traveling secretary.
?

After our snack, we go back to Alain's room to listen to records, well, one record, and to play cowboys and Indians with Napoleon's soldiers.
Then Alain's Mommy comes and tells me that it's time to go and that her husband will take me home.

Alain's Daddy maneuvers his wheelchair like an ace.
And he drives very well.

Interlude

Dear Jean. I'm in Switzerland. I've been skiing all week...
?
But it's summertime!
Not in Switzerland, it's winter there... and stop interrupting me...
The trees are all white with the snow, it's cold...
There, you see!
I bought a cuckoo clock. I'll show it to you when I get back. Love, Mommy.
Is that all?
Well yes, that's it.

Chapter 5: Yvette
Before Yvette there was another woman
who took care of my brother and I.
She was also called Yvette.
She was young,
she was blonde,
she played guitar.

But most of all she played the martinet.

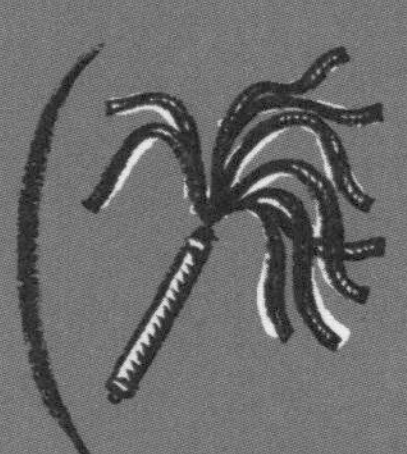

Martinet: multitailed whip used for punishing naughty children. Michele's Daddy uses one on his dogs.

Luckily, Daddy didn't go in for the martinet.

Goodbye Yvette-the-martinet and hello Yvette-chocolate-milk.

Straight away my brother and I liked her a lot.

I think my Daddy also likes Yvette. Yvette likes my Daddy too but she most of all she likes her boyfriend who she sees on the sly.

Her boyfriend's name is Daniel. I met him by chance one afternoon, at the bottom of the yard.

I was playing hide and seek with my brother, and he was hiding too, behind a tree...

?
Shh! Don't be afraid...

I ain't afraid!

Go and tell Yvette that Daniel is waiting for her... But, please, don't tell your Daddy that you saw me, or Yvette will be in trouble. OK?

Another secret wasn't going to make much of a difference.

(Daniel was a fireman at Biscarosse. Some years later, he married Yvette and went away with her to the Landes area. If I'd known that because of him Yvette would leave us two years later, I'd've blown the whistle on him right then and there.)

On top of all her other virtues, Yvette is a great cook.
She subscribes to "Recipe Cards" and tries all the recipes
she receives by mail. We eat...

...cheese soufflés,

stuffed eggplant,

blackberry clafoutis.

You'll soon be ready to get married.

Would you like some more endives with white sauce?

Neither my brother nor I like endives, nor broccoli, nor Brussels sprouts but we eat them all the same because we love Yvette. We love Yvette like she was our Mommy.

Though she is not our Mommy...

MOMMY, I WANT SOME NOODLES!!

Paul, I am not your Mommy.
I am your nanny.

WAAAAHHHH!! I WANT NOOODLES!!!!

In kindergarten last year, the teacher had us make gifts for Mother's Day.

I made a necklace out of macaroni which I painted in different colors and strung on some yarn.

I felt like saying, "Happy Mother's Day, Mommy!" but I just said, "Happy Mother's Day, Yvette!" because I know that she doesn't want to be called Mommy.

She smiled and thanked me but a tear rolled down her cheek.

Interlude
At night, when I wake up, there's a witch sitting beside my bed.
She watches me and if I move, she kills me. So, I don't even bat an eyelid. I try not to breathe so she won't hear me. I keep still.
In the morning, when I open my eyes, she's gone.

Chapter 6: Louis de Funès
What I don't like about school...

...is recess.

- Either you play marbles with your classmates - I love playing marbles with my brother, I always win. But I hate playing marbles with my classmates, I always lose.

- Or you play soccer. I love playing soccer. But my classmates say I'm a lousy kicker and they make me be the goalie...

...and stopping shots hurts.

- Or you talk about what you've watched on TV. I love TV. But in our house, my Daddy won't let us watch it. He says it's not good for school. Anyway, not watching TV is not good for recess.

Hey, d'ya see that funny movie with Funès last night?

Yeah, it was great!

Wasn't it hysterical when he climbed up on the other guy's shoulders !!

It was... Ah, yeh, yeh! Totally!

Did you see it?

Er...yeah...

Hey! Liar! You're not allowed to watch TV in your house!

Yes, I did see it!

Ha! Ha! What a liar!

Happily for us, my brother and I have a system so we can watch TV when Yvette is busy in the kitchen fixing supper and before Daddy comes home from the factory.

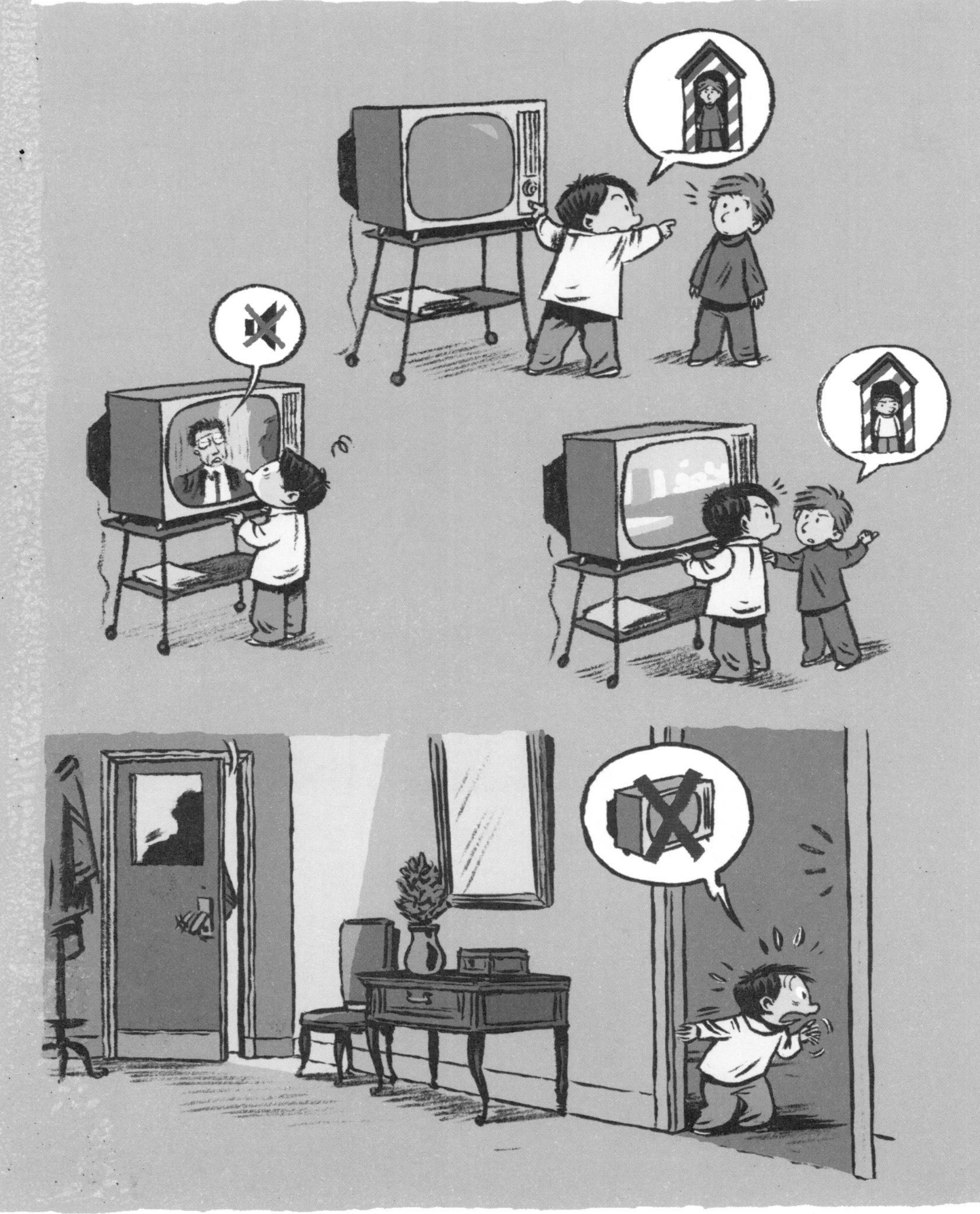

Unhappily, my father has a way of finding out
if we've just switched the TV off.

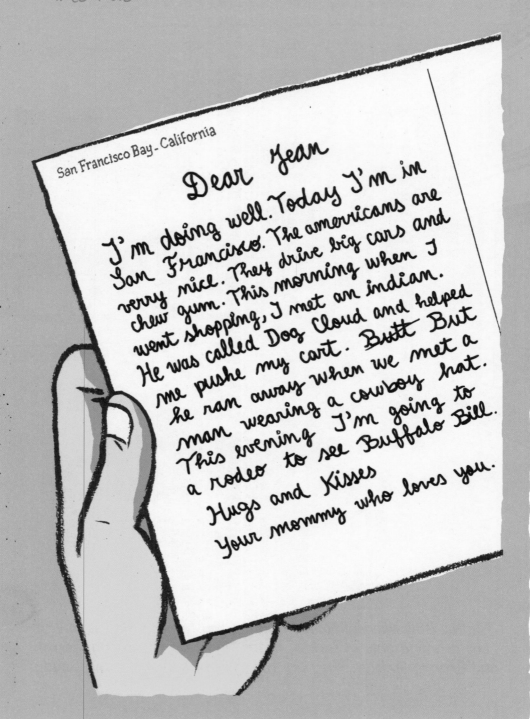

Interlude

San Francisco Bay - California

Dear Jean

I'm doing well. Today I'm in
San Francisco. The amerricans are
verry nice. They drive big cars and
chew gum. This morning when I
went shopping, I met an indian.
He was called Dog Cloud and helped
me pushe my cart. ~~Butt~~ But
he ran away when we met a
man wearing a cowboy hat.
This evening I'm going to
a rodeo to see Buffalo Bill.

Hugs and Kisses
Your mommy who loves you.

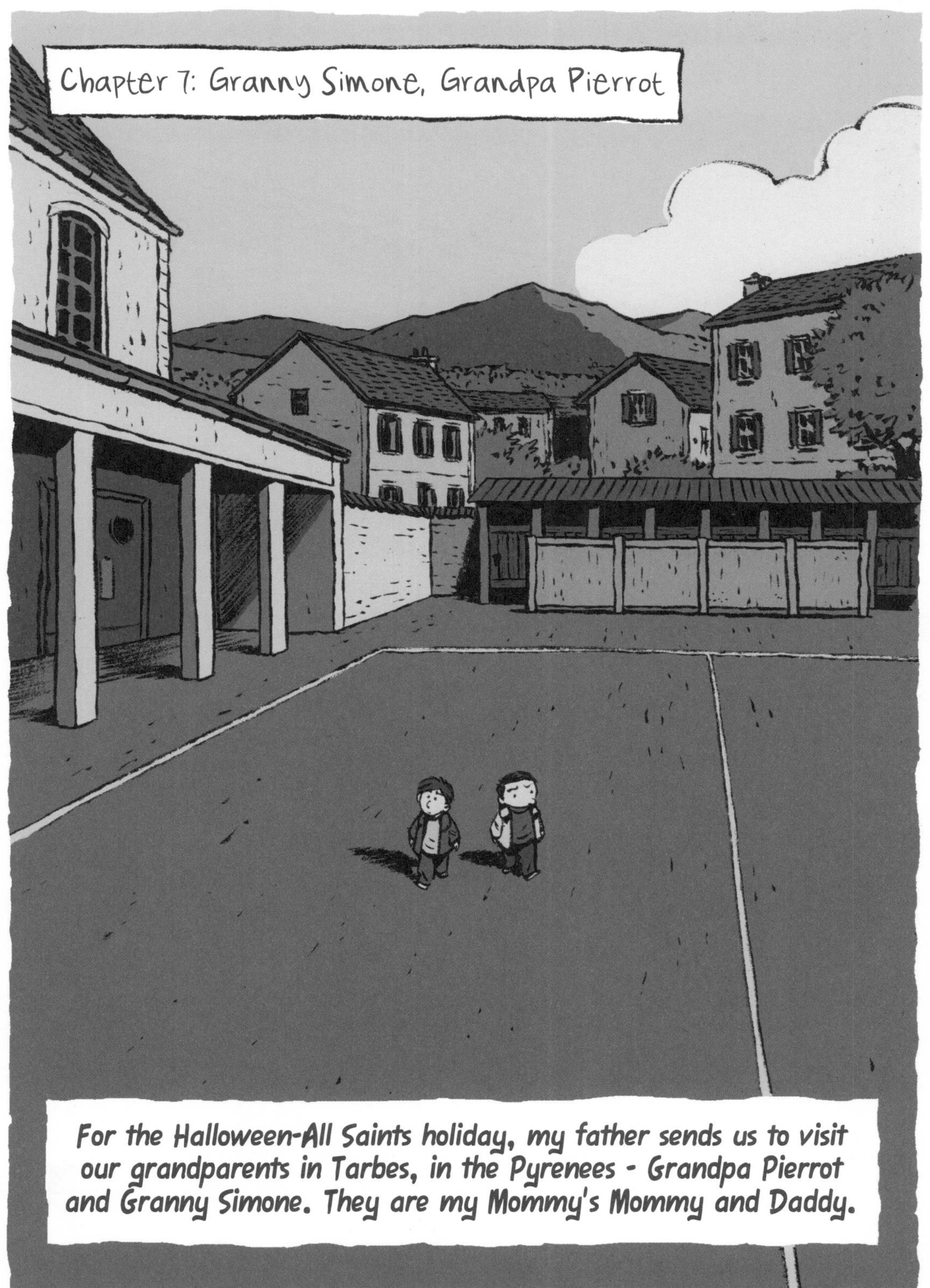
Chapter 7: Granny Simone, Grandpa Pierrot
For the Halloween-All Saints holiday, my father sends us to visit our grandparents in Tarbes, in the Pyrenees - Grandpa Pierrot and Granny Simone. They are my Mommy's Mommy and Daddy.

My brother and I don't like visiting them...

In the first place, Granny is a teacher and they live in a school. It's not much fun spending your holiday in a school...

Secondly, my Granny isn't as good a cook as Yvette. For example, in the morning she gives us hot water with powdered chocolate.

For lunch, an overcooked steak and in the evening, a tough salad dripping with vinegar.

Besides, my Granny isn't as nice as Yvette. In the afternoons she takes us to the park which is really dark and damp.

It stinks of dog poo and cat pee.
We're so bored that time stands still.

Luckily, it rains sometimes so we can stay in and watch cartoons.

But more than anything else, what we hate most when we're in Tarbes are my Grandpa's feet...

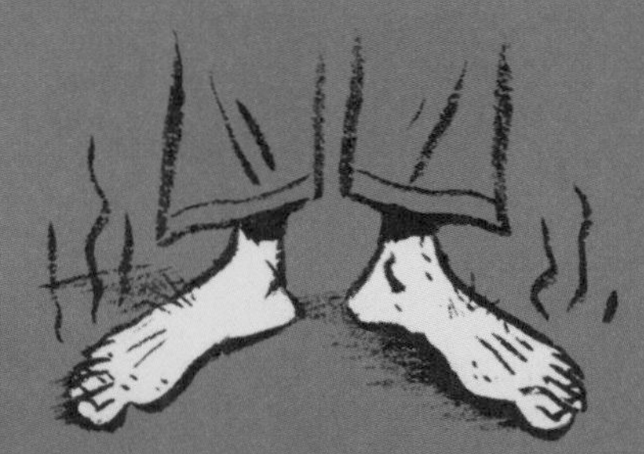

My Grandpa is a draftsman at the gunpowder factory. It must be really hot in there. In the evening, after work, he takes off his shoes and puts on his leather sandals. The smell is very very very bad. It burns your nose and you can't breathe. Sometimes, it stinks so bad that we hide in the closet so as not to smell them.

Above the fireplace there's a painting...
Granny says it's my Mommy. She's wearing a red and white striped tee-shirt and is putting a flower in her hair.
Maybe we should tell them...
That's not up to us...
?

There's things that are worse than the tough salad, the park and Grandpa's smelly feet. Granny's friends.

We run into them everywhere: in the street, in shops, at the sandbox. They are old and prickle when they kiss us. They ruffle our hair and then look at us sadly, like we were sick.

He's the spitting image of his Mommy.

Spitting or splitting image?

One afternoon, on our way back from the Park,
I pitched a fit so my Granny would buy me a tee-shirt...

Interlude

Since my Granny is a teacher, she teaches me to read and write so I can get ahead of my classmates.

During that Halloween-All Saints holiday, I draw thousands of loops, circles, legs, hats, bars.

My brother doesn't feel like learning anything except for the adventures of Dynamo Duck...

...or Pépin the Bubble blower

Chapter 8: Jean-Michel Tong
Monday, November 2, 1970
At school, after the Halloween-All Saints holiday, the teacher introduces a man to us.

She tells us he is a psychologist and that some of us are going to have an appointment with him...

He looks sort of creepy with his dark glasses and short black beard.
I pray I'm not one of the ones who'll have to go see him...

?
At recess, the psychologist comes looking for Pascal Vénert.

Pascal is taller than everyone else. It seems he's two years behind. He's very nice but I overheard his Daddy, who is our mechanic, tell mine that Pascal is not very "quick-witted".

I wonder what "quick-witted" means?

Hey, Yvette! Am I quick-witted?
?

Hmm... I don't know...

If you have to ask, then you surely aren't!
?

After the visit to the psychologist, Pascal didn't return to school!

So where's Pascal gone to?
The teacher said that they're going to send him to the Sess!

What's the Sess?

It's those nasty Germans, who kill everyone!
? ? ? ?

During the war, they set the village of Mouleydier on fire! My father told me!

Duh! No! It's a school where they send those who are a little wacko.

Not quick-witted=wacko

The next day, the psychologist asked to see Jean-Michel Tong.

Jean-Michel is Vietnamese and never says a word, neither in class nor at recess. He smiles all the time when you speak to him. We haven't the foggiest whether he even knows French.

Sometimes, there are kids who make fun of him...

Tong, dirty chink!
Stinkychink Tong!

Lucky for him, he's got two older brothers at school to protect him...

Before the holidays, the teacher had taken us to the swimming pool.

The coach sent those who could swim to the big pool.

♪!

Jean-Michel Tong doesn't have to go to the Sess after all! The day after his visit to the psychologist he even uttered his first words!

So Chinky, they haven't sent you off to the Sess?

You shuddup or I call my brudders!

Interlude

Chapter 9: The Psychologist
Wednesday, November 4, 1970
!!!
Alain is the third one to be called by the psychologist! He wasn't expecting that at all!

As we leave school,
I meet Alain who's coming
back from the psychologist.
He's very pale.

Good grief! They're going to send me off to the Sess!
D'you think so?

I've failed all the tests!!!
What did you have to do?

There were black blobs and I had to say what I saw...
So?

Well, I didn't recognize anything... so I said I saw the sea.
The sea?

Yes. And marines. And then, the shrink asked me a ton of questions about my family. As a matter of fact right now he's talking to my Mommy.

It's the first time I hear
him say "my Mommy" and
not "Sophie" or "my
adoptive mother".

Luckily, the next day Alain's back in class.
I'm really happy to see him...

But my joy is short lived. The teacher calls me...

IT'S MY TURN TO GO TO THE PSYCHOLOGIST!!!

His office is in a sort of trailer which is parked on the playground.

I sit across from the psychologist, petrified. First he makes me count and read some letters.

It's really easy, but then he shows me some little cards with black blobs. These are the pictures Alain told me about!

The psychologist asks me what the blobs remind me of. Frankly, I can't think of anything, but I figure I'll be better off if I give the same answers as Alain. If it worked for him, then it will surely work for me.

Finally, the psychologist asks me to tell him about my last vacation! Shoot! Alain didn't warn me about this!

I immediately thought about the park in Tarbes, the dog poo, my Granny's prickly friends and my Grandpa's sandals. But I doubt he wants to hear about that... So, I tell the psychologist that I went to the United States with my Mommy. That we went shopping in a supermarket and met Indians. I also told him that we went to see a rodeo with Buffalo Bill.

The psychologist asks me if I remember my Mommy clearly.

I answer yes, of course, seeing as how I spent my last vacation with her.

Afterwards, the psychologist makes some notes in his notebook... I tell myself that I shouldn't have made up that story about the rodeo...

Before leaving, I ask him if I'm going to be sent to the Sess.

He looks at me in surprise and says no, that I'm going back to my class along with the rest.

Interlude

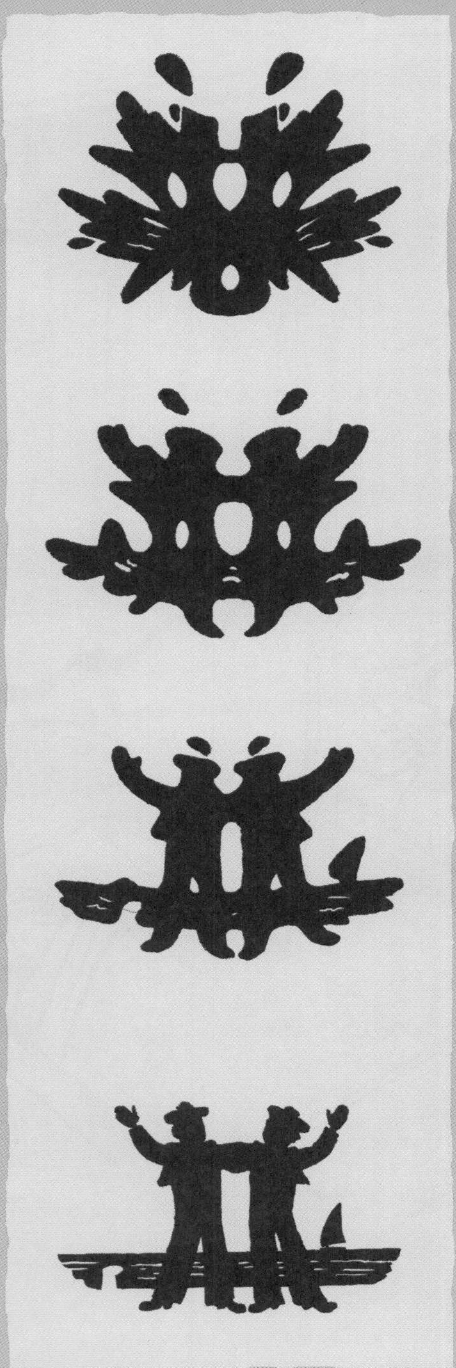

Chapter 10 : My Mommy
That evening, as I fall sleep, a lot of questions pop into my head...

Why did the psychologist want to see me?
What do the black blobs really mean?
Why did he talk about Mommy to me?

Hey, Paul! Are you sleeping?

No! Wanna fight?

D'you... do you remember Mommy?

Um, yes...

What is it you remember?

Um, that she's nice... That she's nice and....

MOMMMMY!

WAAAHHHH!

CLICK!
?
!
?

After Yvette leaves, I start thinking real hard about my Mommy.

What do I remember about her?

I remember...

My memories of Mommy have faded away...
I don't remember anything about her anymore...
Why did she go away on a trip? Why does she write only to me?

All of a sudden I hear a noise in the room next door...

?

I get up and see through the keyhole that Daddy and Yvette are watching a movie...

I CAN WATCH THE TV THROUGH THE KEYHOLE!

Well, at least half the screen...

Tomorrow at last, I'll be able to laugh along with the rest of them at the Bourvil and Funès movies... I'm really happy!

Interlude
Dear Jean.
Now I'm in Africa where, as you know, it is very hot.
The people are all black and you can see their beautiful white
teeth when they laugh. In the forest, there are zebras, giraffes,
lions, tigers and gazelles. I even saw a herd of elephants who
were walking Indian file. If I have room in my case, I will
bring you an elephant's tusk. Kisses.
Your Mommy.
!
Michele forgets to take the postcard back.
I keep it and, in the evening, I slip it
under my mattress.

Chapter 11: The Ossards
?
One Saturday, Yvette tells us that she is taking us to visit the Ossards. My brother and I are baffled.

Who are the Hussars?
They are family friends.
So why don't we know them?
They're old and don't go out often.
?
But they love you very much.
How can somebody I don't know love me?
They don't have any children, it would make them happy to have you over for an afternoon.
?

Me, I'd much rather go and kick a ball around down at the dead-end... and my brother agrees with me. But despite our protests we are put into the Simca 1100.

The Ossards are very old. The lady has a voice that's thin and quivery, the man's is very high-pitched.

We go outdoors and he shows us his rabbits in a hutch down at the bottom of the yard. We tell him we don't like rabbits.

Then the man takes us to see his baby ducks who are going "quack-quack" in a cage. But we don't like ducks either.

So, we go back into the kitchen...

The inside of the house is all gray and glum.
You'd say its color has rubbed off onto the Ossards.

Madame Ossard made us a mountain of pancakes.

It's not really snacktime
but we sit down at
the table...

I remembered that you used to love pancakes.
?

Of course, I was born on Pancake Day.

The two of you, you're both the spitting image...
Elise, come on!

SNIFF!

Madame Ossard must be one of Granny Simone's friends, the kind that sniffle and pat my head.

As a matter of fact...

Aren't they good now?
SCRAT! SCRAT!

Yvette'sh are better.

That day my brother and I totally agreed on everything.

After the pancakes, we insist on watching TV telling them that it's time for the cartoons we watch every Saturday at home. We're a bit disappointed because the TV is black and white but for once in our lives, we spend the whole afternoon watching TV.

At one point, it has the adventures of Dynamo Duck, the little duck all sorts of things happen to.

ROOOO!
ROOOOOHH!

Since the Ossards are napping, that gives us an idea...

On the way home, we cry all the way. We say that the house didn't smell nice, that the pancakes were poisoned and that the people slept with their rabbits...

Yvette doesn't believe us, but we never went back there again!

Interlude

The adventures of Dynamo Duck!

Chapter 12: Granny Edith
At the start of winter, Granny Edith comes to live with us. She's Daddy's Mommy.

She lives in the country, in a big house where we spend almost all our summer vacations. In the winter, when it's cold, she prefers to live with us in town.

Paul and I love Granny Edith. She's very nice to us.

When we are on vacation at her house, she lets us watch TV all the time, we can make noise, we can chase each other around the house, we can have pillow fights, we can make tents in the attic, we can hunt for treasure in the cellar, we can cut bamboo to make arrows, we can play with the neighbors, we can ride bikes...

...even on steep slopes.

Granny Edith is very sweet. She hardly ever uses more than two or three words when she talks. Her favorite phrase is:

Yes, of course!

The only time I ever saw her get annoyed was the day my brother stole a pack of cigarettes to see what it's like to smoke...

Actually, more than anything else, Granny Edith likes for us to stay out of her way. Her three favorite pastimes are: smoking cigarettes, doing crossword puzzles and reading novels with black covers.

Yes, of course...

Today is St. Martin's festival. Granny Edith is also very generous. She gives us some money so we can enjoy ourselves at the fair.

Yvette takes us in the Simca 1100 to the big square where the fair is. My brother wants to go on the merry-go-round. Me, I tell him I'm too big for that!

Still, he looks like he's having a good time, up in that airplane...

When Paul's done, we go over to the bumper-cars. Yvette gets in with Paul, me, I'm all by myself! BING! We bump into each other over and over again!!

What I really like at the fair are the gumball machines. Yvette reads the sign, «Who pleasure gives, Shall joy receive». My brother and I, we prefer to be on the receiving end.

The first time I draw I get some booby traps. I quickly put them in my pocket before Yvette sees them. I'm not yet sure what I'm going to do with them .

Next I get a hairy spider. My brother draws a glow-in-the-dark skeleton and a big ring with a skull. He gives Yvette the ring but she doesn't want it. She suggests he give it to Daddy.

When we get back to the house we try to scare Granny Edith with the spider.

However, at school, the spider is a great success.

Unfortunately I lose it quite quickly at marbles...

Interlude

The List

Daddy checks our list for Father Christmas which we wrote with Granny's help. My brother wants an aquarium with a shark. Daddy thinks that's a good idea but that Father Christmas might prefer to bring him goldfish. My brother cries because he wants a shark, not goldfish.

I want an Indian costume. Daddy asks me if I'm not a bit too old to be playing like that. I didn't know there was an age limit to dressing up as an Indian...

So then I say that I want a S.W.A.T. Team costume.

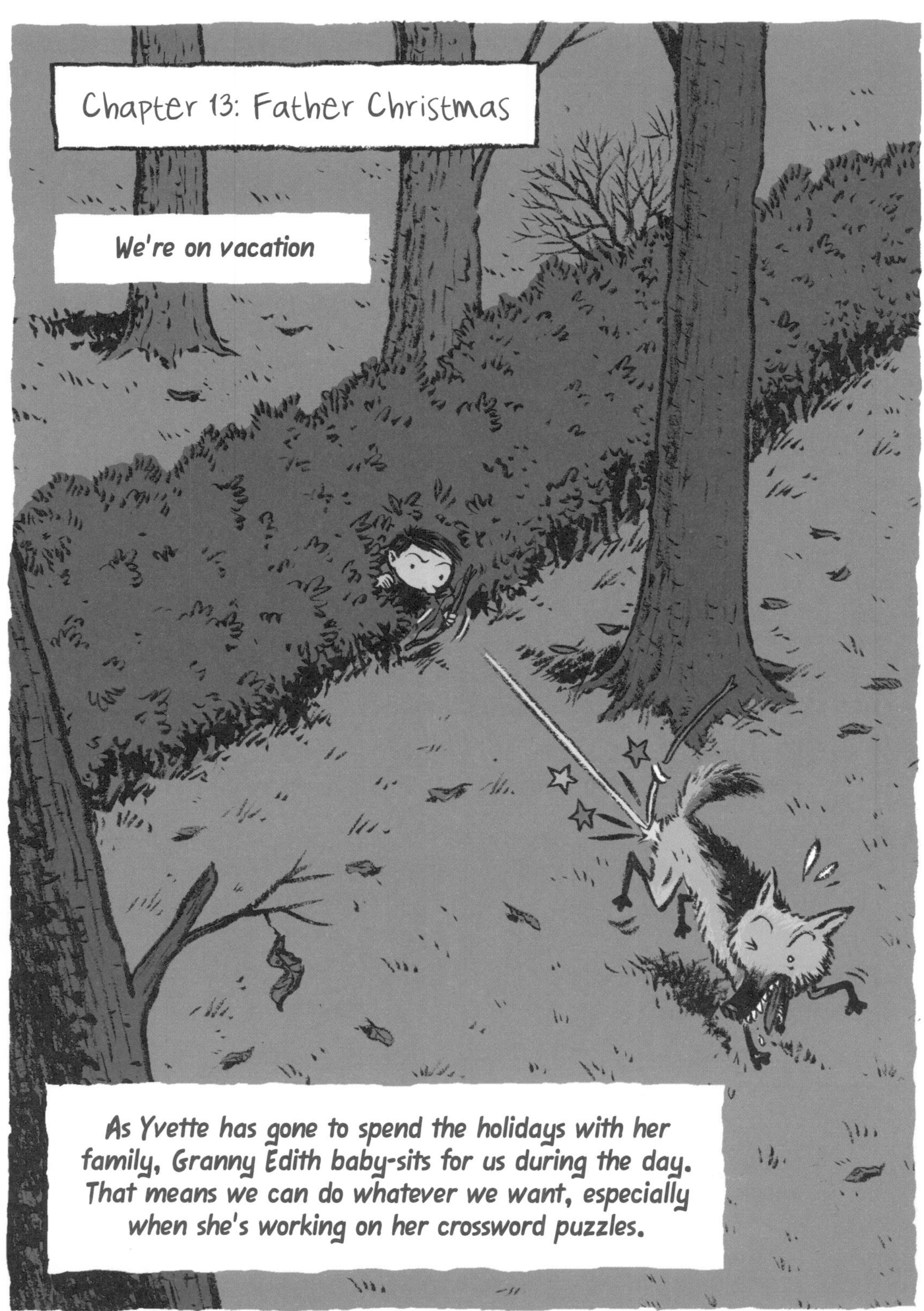
Chapter 13: Father Christmas
We're on vacation
As Yvette has gone to spend the holidays with her family, Granny Edith baby-sits for us during the day. That means we can do whatever we want, especially when she's working on her crossword puzzles.

Today is the eve of the big day... Paul and I, we have a big plan: take a picture of Father Christmas.

My brother has got hold of Daddy's Polaroid camera, which he's hidden under his bed.

That evening, before we go to bed, I ask what time Father Christmas usually comes...

My Daddy frowns. Granny Edith says that no one ever knows the exact time because he has a lot of work and he never comes twice at the same time.

Paul and I go to bed and pretend to be asleep. We can't turn the light on as otherwise my Daddy would realize that we aren't sleeping. We take turns as look out. Through the keyhole we can make out the end of the hallway and part of the Christmas tree next to the TV. The garlands twinkle in the dark.

It's hard to stay awake in the dark. As a matter of fact I fall asleep...

Luckily my brother is more persistent. He wakes me up because he's just heard a noise.

We open the bedroom door very quietly.

THERE IS SOMEONE BY THE CHRISTMAS TREE!!
We move slowly down the hall...
SUDDENLY THE ROOM LIGHTS UP!!
My brother has just pressed on the camera and the flash has gone off!
We hear a big racket as packages fall to the floor and there's a sound of glass shattering.
CRASH!

Then it's dark again...
Next my father appears and lights into us!

He gives us a good scolding because we left our room! He sees the Polaroid. I tell him we wanted to take a picture of Father Christmas.

He grabs the photo we just took.

There's nothing in it, just the tree at the end of the hallway. He laughs and gives it back.

We go back to bed and promise him we will go to sleep...

In bed, before the light is turned off, I look closely at the photo.

My heart pounds in my chest! Down at the bottom, on the left, next to the tree...

...YOU CAN SEE THE TIP OF ONE OF FATHER CHRISTMAS'S SHOES!!!

I keep the secret to myself and hide the photo under my mattress, together with Mommy's postcard.

Interlude
D.. De... Dea...
Dear... Mi... Miq...
Mickey...Mi... chh...
Michele...

Chapter 14: Everyone and me all by myself
It's Christmas Day!
We find our presents under the tree.

My brother has a book on sharks and a note from Father Christmas telling him that in a few days he will receive another present which he wasn't able to bring because it was too heavy.

I get an Indian costume and a book about cowboys.

PAF!

In the afternoon, while my brother is napping,
I go to see Michele and play with her.

But Michele is waiting for one of her friends. She tells me that she doesn't have time to play with me and that, anyway, she's too old to play Indians.

She says that I look silly in my outfit. That irks me.

I ask her what Father Christmas brought her, but she answers that it's none of my business

I tell her that if she'll play with me later, I'll comb her hair now. She agrees.

You know something... I have a secret to tell you.
?
What's it about?

Look...

?

Is that your Christmas tree?

Yes, but look closer... At the bottom on the left...

I don't see a thing.
Yes, look, here!
?

It's Father Christmas's shoe! My brother and I took a picture of it yesterday.
!

HA! HA! HA! HA! HA! HA!
?

Pfff! You nitwit, that's your father's shoe! THERE'S NO Father Christmas!

I start to cry!!!

I pull her hair. She starts yelling. The dogs bark...

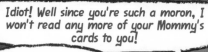

Idiot! Well since you're such a moron, I won't read any more of your Mommy's cards to you!

Huh? Have you got another one?!

Pfff! I'm the one who made your cards up!

YOUR MOTHER IS DEAD!!

I run back to the house in tears.
My father and my Granny can't stop my tears.

When they ask me why I'm crying, I tell them that Michele said that there's no Father Christmas...

He's old enough to know now.

Michele is wrong! Father Christmas does exist but only when you are a child...

...when you grow up, he disappears... You're a big boy now so Father Christmas doesn't exist for you, but he still exists for your brother.

That evening in bed, I tell myself that Mommy is like Father Christmas...
...I'm too old now to believe in her...

Interlude

Epilogue
Goodbye childr
When we go back to school in January, I meet my new teacher. Her name is Madame Méheux. She seems very nice.

She has a big notebook and asks us to tell her our first names...

...only our first names.

Published by Ponent Mon s.l.

Edited by Fanfare

www.ponentmon.com

Translation:
Vanessa Champion and Elizabeth Tierman

Graphic adaptation:
Ill Wind Tidings

ISBN: 978-84-96427-85-3

Printed and bound in Spain by Aleu S.A.

Jean Regnaud was born in the French countryside on pancake day the year that skier Jean-Claude Killey won all those Winter Olympic Gold Medals. Here's what happened after: "I was 3. My grandma, who loved me lots, had bought me a small bag of candy. In among the strawberry tagada and the liquorice heads I discovered a yummy bar of caramel with a yellow and orange wrapper. A wonderful treat which stuck to the teeth a little, it was called *Carambar*. On the inside of the paper were some strange red markings. Intrigued I asked my grandma what they were. She told me it was a form of modern expressionism that was called *writing*. This particular piece was a riddle which she read to me – How did the gardener ripen his tomatoes? - She hesitated a moment, cleared her throat, then read the reply – He stands before them naked to make them turn red! – I remember laughing for hours! In fact, I still tell this joke today. That aside, back then I took an irreversible decision that, one day, I too would learn to use this form of modern expressionism."

On "My Mommy":
"On my very first day in preparatory school, the teacher asked us about the profession of our parents. My Dad was a 'boss' but what about my Mum? I didn't know anything about her. What was her job? What did she look like? Where did she live? Children hate being different from others. So I invented."

Jean Regnaud

Émile Bravo was born in 1964 in Paris of Spanish parents exiled in France. While still a kid, Bravo started sketching on everything (including the family album!) until someone bought him some paper. In school he passed through various "careers" in science including chemist (the nitro-glycerine was fun), engineer (he loved trains) and Einstein (E=mc2 – nothing is lost, only transformed – an idea he used later in his successful series *Jules*). At 19 he changed horizon and enrolled in a course on History of Art so he could get his student discount at the movie theatres. Working part-time at *Marie-France* he pursued his passion for comics in his spare time. It was this period which produced *Ivoire*, his first collaboration with his friend Regnaud. In 1992 he joined a studio which included Tronheim, Sfar and David B and started work with Regnaud on the popular series *Aleksis Strogonov*. In 1999 he started his juvenile series *Jules* about an adolescent chosen to go on an expedition to explore Alpha Centauri, which has been described as *Tin Tin* for the 21st Century. Book 2 in the series, *The Unexpected Republic*, won him the *Prix Goscinny* at the Angoulême Festival, France in 2001. A recent short story *Young Americans*, which appeared in Fantagraphics' *Mome #8*, earned him an Eisner nomination in 2008.

On "My Mommy":
"Jean Regnaud has been a dear friend since adolescence so, when he showed me this text, I was truly moved ... it was astonishing! Jean, with tremendous modesty, had performed the miracle of narrating a most tragic aspect of his childhood. He causes laughter without cynicism and rouses deep emotions without feeling pity. I hope I was able to find a graphic style to complement his story."

Émile Bravo